SESAME STREET

Hooray for Our Heroes!

By Sarah Albee • Illustrated by Tom Brannon

A Random House PICTUREBACK® Book
Random House 🏛 New York

Text and illustrations copyright © 2002 Sesame Workshop. Sesame Street Muppet characters copyright © 2002 Sesame Workshop.
All rights reserved under International and Pan-American Copyright Conventions.
Published in the United States by Random House Children's Books, a division of Random House, Inc., New York, and
simultaneously in Canada by Random House of Canada Limited, Toronto, in conjunction with Sesame Workshop.
Sesame Street, Sesame Workshop, and their logos are trademarks and service marks of Sesame Workshop.
Library of Congress Control Number: 2002141057
ISBN: 0-375-82268-2
Printed in the United States of America 10 9 8 7 6 5 4 3 2 1
www.randomhouse.com/kids/sesame
www.sesamestreet.com
PICTUREBACK, RANDOM HOUSE, and the Random House colophon are registered trademarks
and the Please Read to Me colophon is a trademark of Random House, Inc.

Hello there, everybodee! It is I, your furry superhero pal, Super Grover! Today I am going to tell you what the word "hero" means. A hero is someone who you see in comic books and cartoons. Heroes are make-believe.

First of all, a hero has a special uniform, similar to the outfit that I am wearing, with a cape on the back and a letter on the chest. I do not see anyone else wearing a hero uniform, do you?

And, of course, everyone knows that heroes have very large muscles and are very strong. No one around *here* is especially strong.

Heroes move with lightning speed. No one around *here* can do that.

Of course, heroes must also be able to fly. Aside from yours truly, no one around *here* can do that.

And heroes must be able to leap tall buildings in a single bound.

Heroes are famous. They are never the people that we see walking around our own neighborhoods.

My best friend is my hero! He taught me how to ride a bike.

How would you know a hero if you saw one? That is a very good question! And I, Grover, will answer it for you. For starters, heroes definitely do not wear glasses.

And heroes do not just sit around, waiting for things to happen.

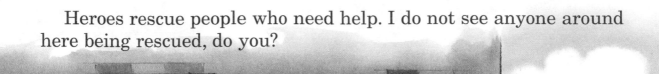

Heroes rescue people who need help. I do not see anyone around here being rescued, do you?

Heroes are people you look up to.

Heroes protect and defend.